CAT GAMES

For Janet Schulman

PUFFIN BOOKS
Published by the Penguin Group
Penguin Books USA Inc., 375 Hudson Street, New York, New York 10014, U.S.A.
Penguin Books Ltd, 27 Wrights Lane, London W8 5TZ, England
Penguin Books Australia Ltd, Ringwood, Victoria, Australia
Penguin Books Canada Ltd, 10 Alcorn Avenue, Toronto, Ontario, Canada M4V 3B2
Penguin Books (N.Z.) Ltd, 182-190 Wairau Road, Auckland 10, New Zealand

Penguin Books Ltd, Registered Offices: Harmondsworth, Middlesex, England

First published in the United States of America by Viking,
a division of Penguin Books USA Inc., 1988
Published simultaneously in Puffin Books
Published in a Puffin Easy-to-Read edition, 1995

9 10 8

Text copyright © Harriet Ziefert, 1988
Illustrations copyright © Claire Schumacher, 1988
All rights reserved

Puffin® and Easy-to-Read® are registered trademarks of Penguin Books USA Inc.

The Library of Congress has cataloged the Puffin Books edition as follows:
Ziefert, Harriet.
Cat games / Harriet Ziefert; pictures by Claire Schumacher.
p. cm.—(Hello Reading!; 7)
Summary: Two cats, Matt and Pat, play hide and seek and a chasing game.
ISBN 0-14-050809-0
[1. Cats—Fiction. 2. Hide-and-seek—Fiction. 3. Games—Fiction.]
I. Schumacher, Claire, ill. II. Title. III. Series: Ziefert, Harriet.
Hello Reading! (Puffin Books); 7.
PZ7.Z487Cat 1988b [E]—dc19 87-25805 CIP AC

Puffin Easy-to-Read ISBN 0-14-037885-7

Printed in the United States of America

Reading Level 1.3

CAT GAMES

Harriet Ziefert
Pictures by Claire Schumacher

PUFFIN BOOKS

Chapter One
Hide-and-Seek

Where are the cats?

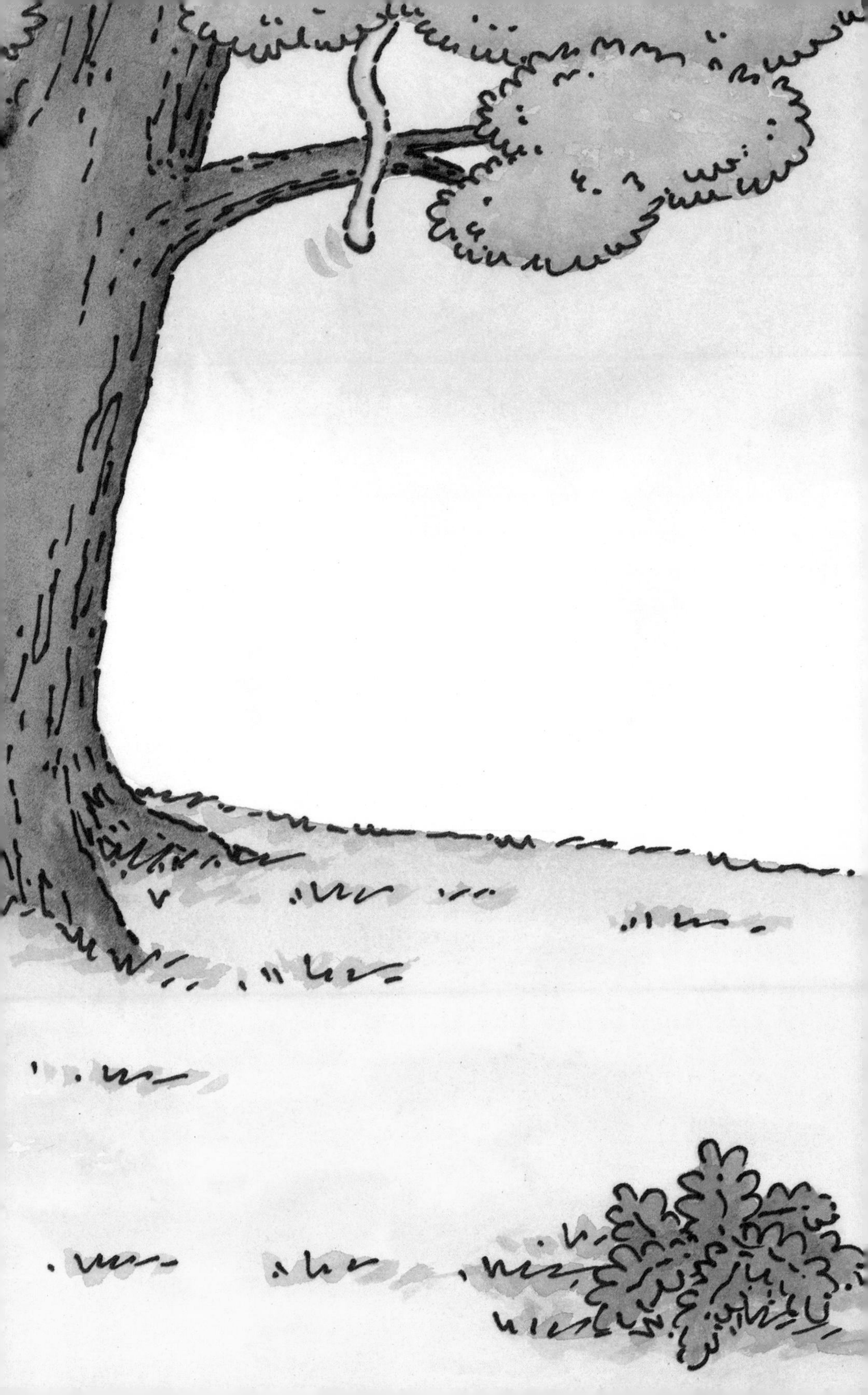

One orange cat
up in a tree.
One gray cat
under a tree.

Up in a tree is Pat.
Under the tree is Matt.
Matt calls.
He wants Pat to come down.

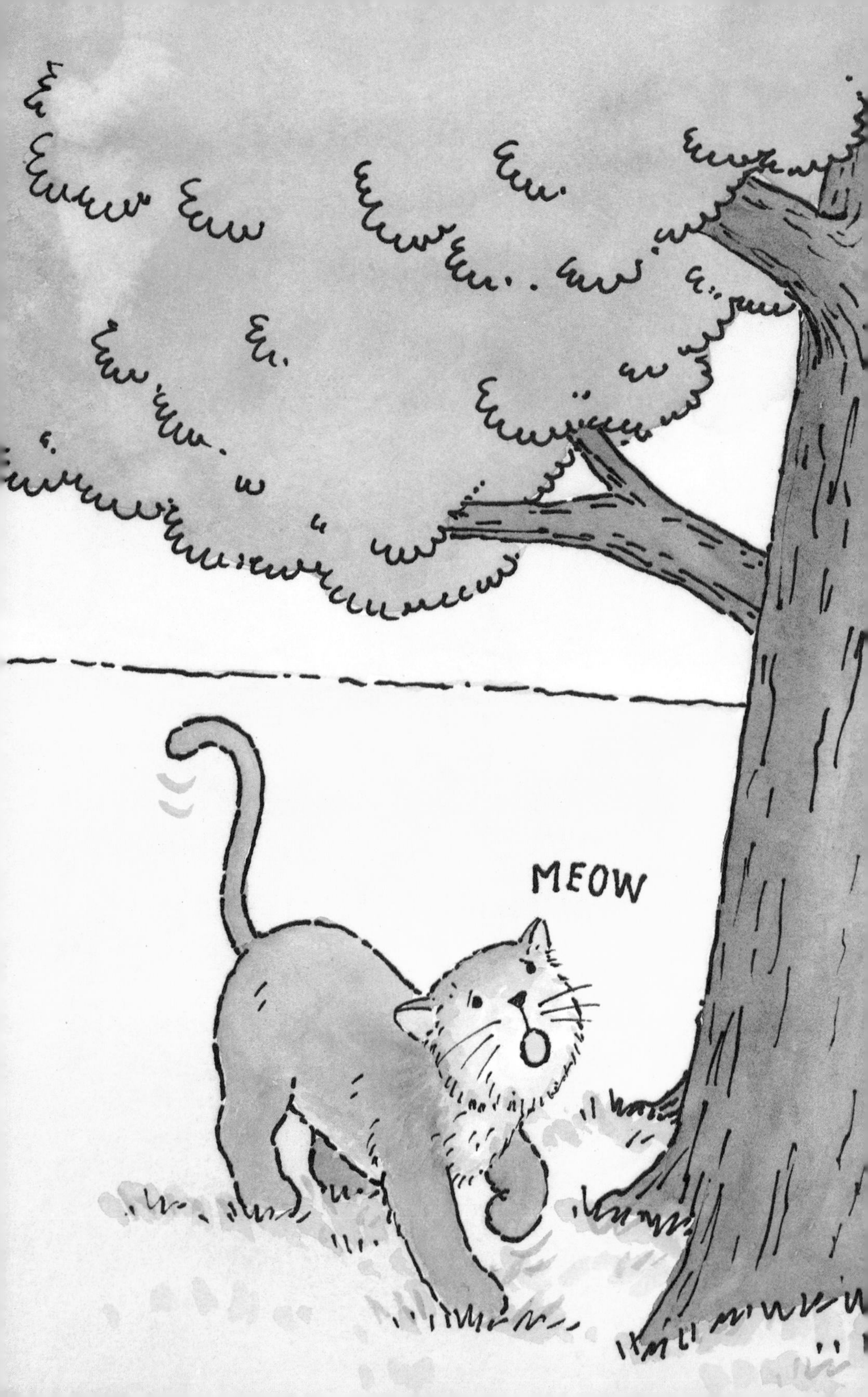
MEOW

Pat looks down at Matt.
Then she jumps higher!

One cat still up in the tree.
One cat still under the tree.
Up in the tree is she.
Under the tree is he.

Matt calls again.
He wants Pat to come down.
But she wants to go higher.

MEOW

Pat jumps again!

Now Matt can't see Pat.
So he climbs up the tree.

Pat hides.

Matt seeks.

Two cats play
hide-and-seek.

Where is she?
Where is he?

Where is the gray cat?
Where is the orange cat?
Can you see them?

Chapter Two
New Game

Two cats play
a new game.

Pat runs.
Matt runs after her.

Matt chases Pat
around and around.

Matt runs.
Pat runs after him.

Pat chases Matt
around and around.

Along comes a barking dog.
He chases Matt and Pat.

Up the tree runs Matt.
Up the tree runs Pat.

Under the tree is
the barking dog.
He wants to play.
The dog looks up
at Pat and Matt.

Pat and Matt look down
at the dog.

Pat looks at Matt.
Matt looks at Pat.

They look up and down.
And then...

they jump!

Two cats
and a dog
play under a tree!